Little Jack Rabbit and Uncle John Hare

David Cory

LITTLE JACK RABBIT AND UNCLE JOHN HARE

UNCLE JOHN HARE

"Heigh-ho," said Little Jack Rabbit to himself one bright morning, "how happy I'd be if I could find Uncle John Hare." And then, all of a sudden he came to a sign by the road on which was printed in big red letters:

"THREE MILES TO TURNIP CITY"

"Perhaps someone there can tell me where he lives," and the little rabbit set out with a brave heart once more, and pretty soon, not so very far, he came to a little house painted white, with green shutters and a red chimney. And, goodness me! Before he could say "Winky pinky" Uncle John Hare himself opened the door.

"How did you get here all by yourself? It's a long way from the Old Bramble Patch," inquired the old gentleman rabbit.

Well, you can imagine how glad the little tired bunny was to find his uncle, and for a long time he for got to ask him how he came to leave the Sunny Meadow, and why he had bought this little house in Turnip City. But, by and by, his uncle explained it all by saying he wished to pass the rest of his days in quiet, far away from the Farmer's Boy and Danny Fox.

"Now come around to the back of the house and I'll show you my little garage," said the old gentleman bunny. "I have a Bunnymobile that goes so fast you can't count the miles before you are home again." Wasn't that a wonderful automobile to have? Well, I just guess it was. And after the little rabbit had looked it over his uncle took him back in the house and showed him the little room which was to be his as long as he lived in Turnip City.

"Won't we have fine times together!" said the old gentleman rabbit, with a laugh. "I've been waiting for just this happy moment. You and I can travel all over together in sunshiny, snow-falling, rain-wetting weather." And he slapped the little bunny's back and gave a hop, skip and jump to one side, and then laughed some more, for he was as happy as a clam at high tide, as an old fisherman used to say when I was a boy not so very long ago, but just long enough to make me wish I were twenty years younger, just the samee.

Well, after a while, it was bedtime, and the cuckoo came out of her little clock-house and said:

"Time for bed, you sleepy head,Don't sit up too late.It won't be long before my songWill make the clock strike eight."

And in the next story you shall hear what happened after that.

A USEFUL GUMDROP

The next morning when Little Jack Rabbit woke up for a moment he forgot he was in Uncle John Hare's house, Turnip City, U.S.A. But in less than five hundred short seconds he knew where he was, when the cuckoo came out of her little clock-house and sang:

"Wake up, wake up! It's early morn,The sun is sparkling the dew on the corn,The little field mouse is looking aboutAnd the little red rooster's beginning to shout,"

and his kind rabbit uncle looked in at the door and said:

"The buckwheat cakes are sizzling hot,The maple sugar's sweet,So hurry up and dress yourselfSo we'll have time to eat."

Well, you can just bet your last Liberty bond coupon the little bunny didn't linger in bed, but dressed himself as fast as a fireman and was down at the breakfast table before his uncle had eaten more than thirteen buckwheat cakes.

As soon as the old gentleman rabbit's housekeeper, Mrs. Daisy Duck, had cleared away the table and made out a list for the grocer, these two happy rabbits hopped into the Bunnymobile and started off for Turnip City to buy sugar and flour and maybe a bag of animal crackers.

Well, they had gone only just so far when they met little Red Riding Hood on her way to her grandmother's.

"Jump in and we'll save you maybe a mile," said the old gentleman rabbit. "But we must keep a sharp lookout for Mr. Wicked Wolf!" So in jumped little Red Riding Hood and then off they went. But, oh dear me! In a little while they saw the big bad wolf creeping along among the trees.

"Never mind," said the old gentleman rabbit. "He won't dare touch us while we're in the Bunnymobile!" But just the same he felt a little bit worried, let me tell you, and so would you and so would I if we met a wolf out automobiling.

"We'll play a little trick on him," said the old gentleman rabbit, and he opened his tool box and took out a gumdrop as large as a baseball. "Now if he comes too near I'll throw it to him and he'll snap it up, and before he knows it his long teeth will be stuck in so tight he won't be able to open his mouth for a week and a month!" And the next minute this is just what happened.

"Here's a little gumdrop for you," said the old gentleman rabbit. And the ugly wolf snapped it up in his teeth. But when he tried to open his mouth he couldn't. All he could do was to try to get it out with his paws, and in the next story you will hear what happened after that.

THE RAGGED RABBIT GIANT

Oh, the Bunnymobile's a wonderful car;It goes just as fast as a swift shooting star,And every one says, with a toss of his capThat Uncle John Hare's a lucky old chap.

And now you remember how the last story ended; although in case you don't I'll tell you. Little Jack Rabbit was riding with his dear uncle, Mr. John Hare, of Turnip City, U. S. A.

Well, pretty soon they stopped in front of a grocery store and Little Red Riding Hood, who was with them, you remember, jumped out and went to call on her grandmother, who lived in a little house in the wood.

"Now, let me see," said the old gentleman rabbit, taking out of his pocket the piece of paper on which his housekeeper, Mrs. Daisy Duck, had written the things she wanted him to buy at the grocery store:

"I want a pound of chocolate prunes,Four dozen ice cream cones,A pound or two of sugar glueSome raisins without stones."

"Here they are, Mr. John Hare," said the saleslady, who was a slim young tabby cat, and she handed him the package nicely done up with pink ribbons. So off went the two little rabbits in their Bunnymobile. But, oh, dear me! On their way home whom should they meet but the Ragged Rabbit Giant of the Skyhigh Mountain. He had just climbed down to take a look over Turnip City, which is on the other side of the Sippi River, you know.

"Hey, hey!" he shouted. "Where are you going?"

"I guess I'd better stop," said the old gentleman rabbit. "I don't want to be impolite, but neither do I want to be foolhardy, and it certainly is risky talking to a giant." But, oh, dear me; while he was thinking this over the Ragged Rabbit Giant took one long step and stood beside them.

"Well, well, well," he said with a low bow, "if this isn't the little bunny who once made me a visit."

And then he laughed so loud that the trees trembled. "What have you got in that paper bag tied up so nicely?" And he stretched out his big hand to take it, when the old gentleman rabbit made the Bunnymobile horn go off just like a gun which so frightened the Giant Rabbit that he put his fingers to his ears and shut his eyes. And before you could say Jack Robinson the old gentleman bunny started up the Bunnymobile and was almost home when the giant opened them again. And in the next story you shall hear what happened after that.

JACK SPRITE

"Oh, dear me," said Mrs. Daisy Duck, Uncle John Hare's old lady housekeeper, you know, "why don't they get home?" and she looked up and down the road, but she couldn't see the Bunnymobile anywhere.

"Oh, dear, oh, dear, I feel so queer,I wonder what can be the matter;It's quarter past eight and supper is late;I'm so worried I'll never grow fatter."

And then that kind-hearted, anxious duck went into the kitchen to see if the lollypop cookies were burning. And just then, all of a sudden, she heard the honk! honk! of the Bunnymobile horn and she gave a quack of relief and made the turnip tea.

"Ha, ha," said Uncle John Hare, stepping into the kitchen. "Sorry we are late, but we met the Ragged Rabbit Giant on our way home and were detained." Well, pretty soon he and Little Jack Rabbit sat down to supper, and when that was over they both went into the sitting room and made the pianograph play a new tune.

But just then, all of a sudden, they heard a little voice at the keyhole, such a tiny little low voice that at first the little rabbit hardly heard it.

Again the tiny voice came through the keyhole:

"Open the door and let me inI'm hardly as tall as a little tin pin."

"Who are you?" asked Uncle John Hare, getting up from his chair and going over to the door. And then the little voice spoke again. "I'm little Jack Sprite."

So the old gentleman bunny opened the door, and there stood the prettiest little fairy you ever saw. He was dressed in blue, with a tiny green cap on his head, and long pointed turned up shoes.

"I suppose you wonder what brings me here," he said, bowing very politely. "Well, I'll tell you. Somebody has broken the jack-in-the-pulpit flower I live in, and while I was looking for a new home I spied the little light in your window. So I said to myself, 'Perhaps it's a firefly's lantern, then, maybe, it isn't, but I'll go and find out.'"

Then little Jack Sprite hopped up on a chair and crossed his legs. But goodness me. He didn't half fill the chair, although it was the smallest one in the house.

And maybe he would have fallen asleep by and by if the two little rabbits hadn't sent him upstairs to bed, and in the next story you shall hear what happened in the middle of the night.

THE WOODLAND ELF

The little gray mouse came out of her houseJust at the hour of twelve.And what she saw on the moonlit floorWas a tiny woodland elf.

"S-s-sh!" he said, as the little mouse blinked her eyes, frightened, I suppose, at seeing such a strange sight. "Don't wake up the little rabbit."

"What do you want?" asked the little mouse. "Mr. John Hare is very kind to me, and I don't want anything to happen to him."

"Ha, ha!" laughed the little elf, only very low, of course, so as not to be heard. "How could I hurt a big rabbit?"

"I'm not so sure about that," replied the little mouse. "Sometimes little things are more dangerous than big ones," and she tried to look very wise instead of a little bit frightened.

"Don't be worried," said the elf, "I'll tell you why I'm here. Jack Sprite, who lives in a jack-in-the-pulpit flower in the wood, is asleep upstairs. I must see him before the big red rooster crows at three o'clock."

"Mercy me," said the little mousie. "I didn't know there was a fairy upstairs. What's this house coming to? A fairy upstairs and a fairy downstairs. The first thing you know there'll be a giant in the garage."

"Never mind," whispered the elf, walking over to the door. "I must go upstairs and wake Jack Sprite. Otherwise something dreadful is going to happen." And so up he climbed on his tiptoes to the spare room where the little fairy lay asleep in a big feather bed.

"Gracious me!" said the elf to himself. "I shall have to climb up the bedpost," and up he went like a telephone man, only of course he didn't have any spikes in the heels of his shoes. And it was just as well he didn't, for he certainly would have scratched off all the nice varnish.

"Twinkle, twinkle, firefly, like a lantern in the sky," he sang, very soft and low. And pretty soon Jack Sprite opened his eyes and when he saw the little elf, wasn't he surprised.

"Come, Jack, you must be quick. The Ragged Rabbit Giant is gathering all the Jack-in-the-pulpit flowers and pretty soon there won't be one left."

"But how can I stop him?"

"Come with me," said the little elf. "I'll help you." So they both opened the window and slid down a moonbeam. Well, pretty soon, the little gray mouse grew impatient. So she ran upstairs to see what they were about, and in the next story you shall hear what happened after that.

"fee, fie!"

"The moonlight shone on the bedroom floorAs the little gray mouse peeked in through the door,

But the little fairy I told you aboutHad opened the windows and just gone out.So the little gray mouse had nothing to doBut close it again to keep out the flu."

Then she softly stole downstairs so as not to waken Little Jack Rabbit, and after eating a cheese sandwich went to bed. And now I suppose you are wondering what became of the little elf and the tiny fairy I mentioned in the story before this. Well, I'll tell you right away. As soon as they slid off the moonbeam, they scampered away to the forest where the big Ragged Rabbit Giant was stealing all the Jack-in-the-pulpit flowers he could lay hands on.

"Now hide behind this tree and I'll creep under this bush," said the little elf, "and when the Ragged Rabbit Giant comes by you blow your policeman's whistle and I'll blow mine, and I guess that will so frighten him that he'll never come here again."

Pretty soon, not so very long, they heard a sharp crashing of branches and a big thumping on the ground, and then, all of a sudden, the Ragged Rabbit Giant appeared.

"Fee, fie, china and delf,I smell the blood of a little elf,Fie, fee, left, right,I smell the blood of a little sprite."

And, goodness me. Little Jack Sprite and the tiny elf were so frightened that they almost forgot to blow their policeman whistles. And I guess they would have if a little round-eyed owl hadn't tooted:

"Blow your whistles quick I say,And frighten this Rabbit Giant away!"

Goodness me, again! Then how they did blow their whistles, and the Giant almost jumped through his collar, and before you could say Jack Robinson, ran back to his castle and climbed into his big folding bed.

"Now I guess our Shady Forest will be as quiet as Philadelphia," said the tiny elf. And little Jack Sprite said, "Maybe he has left one Jack-in-the-pulpit flower in which I can make my home." Then they both came out from their hiding places and before very long, just a little while, Jack found a Jack-in-the-pulpit flower. So he was all right and as happy as could be, and as the little elf had a home in a big oak tree, he said good-by and ran away just as the little Red Rooster began to crow.

THE OLD WITCH

"Come, let's go for a ride in the Bunnymobile," said Uncle John Hare.

"The wind is blowing from the west,And I've got on my new pink vest,We'll go through Fairy Land, I guess,Maybe a thousand miles or less."

And the old gentleman bunny curled his whiskers and winked at Mrs. Daisy Duck, his old lady housekeeper.

"Well, be sure and get back in time for supper," she said as he and Little Jack Rabbit hopped into the Bunnymobile and rode away.

By and by, after a while, and a laugh and a smile, they came to a queer little house in the wood, so the two little rabbits hopped out and knocked on the door, which was opened by a little girl dressed in blue.

"Good morning," she said, with a courtesy. "Come in and see grandmother." Now her grandmother was a witch, but one of those nice kind witches you seldom hear about. She didn't have a crooked nose, nor a turned-up chin, and her back wasn't humped at all. She really was very nice-looking, indeed, for her blue eyes were kind and her voice sweet and low.

"What can I do for you two gentlemen bunnies?" she asked, taking up her knitting and making the needles fly so fast that they wondered how she could keep from making a slip now and then, and sometimes oftener.

"We're looking for strawberries," answered Little Jack Rabbit.

"Oh, ho!" said the nice old witch, "so that's what you're after. Don't you know that this isn't the time of year for strawberries?"

"I thought they grew all the year 'round in Fairy Land," said Uncle Hare.

"Well, I know where you may find some, but you'll have to sweep away the snow," said the nice old witch. "Go down to the meadow by the River Sippi, and then up a little hill, on the top of which stands a tiny house. Knock on the door and ask Tim Woodman to show you his strawberry patch."

"Thank you," said Uncle John Hare, and he drove away with his little nephew and by and by they came to the little house. And sure enough, when they knocked on the door, Tim Woodman opened it. But goodness me! When they told him what they wanted, he didn't seem at all pleased. I guess he wanted the strawberries for himself. But anyway, when kind Uncle John Hare offered to give him a ride in the Bunnymobile, Tim led them around to the rear of his house, and taking a broom began to sweep away the snow. And in the next story you shall hear what happened after that.

STRAWBERRIES

Tim Woodman swept away the snowTo find his strawberry patch.Just then the wind began to blow

And broke his back door latch.

"Botheration!" said Tim. "I'll have to make a new one!" Just then a little snow fairy jumped out from behind a bush and said: "Brush away the snow, Tim Woodman, and you'll find red, ripe strawberries." And sure enough he found them, and picking a quart, or maybe more, he said:

"Tell the witch within the woodI really gave you all I could."

"You are very kind," said Uncle John Hare. "Tomorrow we'll come and take you for a ride in the Bunnymobile." And then the two little rabbits rode away, carefully holding the box of strawberries, and pretty soon they came to their little house, where Mrs. Daisy Duck, their old housekeeper, was waiting for them.

Goodness me! I wish you could have seen the strawberry shortcake she made for supper. But perhaps it's just as well you couldn't, for I'm not sure you would have been invited to have a piece.

Well, the next morning Little Jack Rabbit and Uncle John Hare set off again in the Bunnymobile, and after they had gone for maybe a mile or more they came to a cave, outside of which sat a queer little dwarf dressed in green, with a red-peaked hat on his head. His long white beard was covered with snowflakes and his bright black eyes twinkled merrily.

"Hello, little rabbits," he called out. "What are you doing so far away from the Old Bramble Patch, U. S. A.?"

"We are visiting Fairy Land," answered Little Jack Rabbit.

"Well, come in and see my tame mice," said the little dwarf, and he shook the snow from his beard and opened a little door. The two little rabbits hopped out of the Bunnymobile and followed him into the cave. Goodness me! You should have seen all the tame mice. Some were white, and some were gray, but they were all dressed up like little men—boots and breeches, coats and hats, and one little mouse carried a cane. I guess he was the leader of these little mice men, for they all seemed to do just exactly what he did.

"I never would have invited you in," said the little dwarf, "if I hadn't trusted you not to tell the Farmer's big Black Cat."

"Ha, ha!" laughed Uncle John Hare, "I don't believe Black Cat has caught a mouse since Little Jack Rabbit kicked him over."

And this made the dwarf smile, for he had just read about it in a book called "Little Jack Rabbit's Adventures." But he didn't have time to say so to Uncle John Hare, for just then the little mice began to sing the song you shall hear in the next story.

MRS. ANT

Now let's put our heads together and try to think where we left off in the last story. Oh, yes, now I remember. Little Jack Rabbit and Uncle John Hare were in the Dwarf's cave listening to the little mice sing about crackers and cheese.

"We are the mice of the little dwarf king,Who has taught us so well the way to sing;Tra la la la, to ro la loo,The rose is red and the violet blue."

When they had finished Little Jack Rabbit gave them a big piece of cheese and said good-by to the dwarf, and after he and Uncle John Hare had gone for maybe a mile, the Bunnymobile all of a sudden, just like that, stopped right in the middle of the road and wouldn't go a step further.

"What's the matter now, I wonder," asked the old gentleman rabbit

"You nearly ran over me," said a little voice, and there stood a tiny ant, dressed in a pink calico gown and a purple sunbonnet.

"Goodness me!" exclaimed Uncle John Hare, "it's a good thing the Bunnymobile saw you in time, because I didn't. Maybe I'd better buy myself some farsighted goggles."

"Where are you going, Mrs. Ant?" piped in the little rabbit.

Now it happened that she was going to the baker shop in Antville which was three miles away, and so were the two little rabbits, so all three started off again, and by and by, they stopped in front of the bakery shop.

"Thank you very kindly, gentlemen," said Mrs. Ant, "it would have taken me a long time to have walked those three miles. Maybe some day I can do you a good turn!" And dropping them a courtesy, she went in to buy a cookie and maybe a jelly tart.

"Where shall we go now?" asked the old gentleman bunny, putting on his goggles and pulling up his coat collar, for it was pretty cold and Mr. North Wind was whistling through the forest.

"Let's go down to the pond to skate," said Little Jack Rabbit, and off they went, but, oh dear me, just as they were strapping on their skates, who should come along but Mr. Wicked Wolf. And poor Uncle John Hare had only one skate on.

"Oh, Mr. Wolf, don't bother me,For somebody's hiding behind the tree,He's looking for you with a great big gun,Perhaps he's the Big Kind Farmer's Son,"

shouted Little Jack Rabbit. But Mr. Wicked Wolf didn't care. And in the next story you shall hear what he said.

MORE ADVENTURES

"Ha, ha!" growled Mr. Wicked Wolf as he looked at the little rabbits. "Which one shall I eat, for they both look sweet, dressed in their pretty fur habits."

"You won't eat either one of us," said Little Jack Rabbit, taking his popgun from his knapsack. "Do you remember what happened to your brother when he tried to kill little Red Riding Hood?"

"Never mind," replied the big beast, creeping toward the Bunnymobile, "I've learned a lot about fighting since that time." And he crept still closer. But the little rabbit never winked an eyelash; he just waited till the wicked animal was close enough to shoot off his left ear.

"Oh, dear, oh, dear! I've lost an earWhat shall I ever do?I never thought I would be caughtAnd made to look so queer."

And that unhappy wolf turned tail and ran away.

"Well, that was a narrow escape," said the old gentleman rabbit. "I don't feel much like sightseeing. Let's turn the Bunnymobile around and get away from here. This old wolf might come back with his brother."

So off they went, and by and by whom should they meet but Prof. Jim Crow sitting on a fence.

"Goodness me!" exclaimed Little Jack Rabbit, "he looks just like that naughty bird who when

The maid was in the garden,Hanging out the clothes,Hopped along the clotheslineAnd nipped off her nose."

"But you know I'm not that bird," he answered, flapping his wings. "It was a cousin of mine. Will you give me a ride in your Bunnymobile? I'll tell you something nice if you do."

"All right, jump in," said the old gentleman rabbit. "What's the nice thing you mention?"

"Not very far from here lives a little yellow hen in a green house. I've heard that she has a magic china egg which is as good as a wishing stone. All you have to do is to hold it in your hand and make a wish and the wish comes true."

"Let's make her a visit," said Little Jack Rabbit, and off they all went to the yellow hen's house and if they reach there I will tell you all about this wonderful wishing egg in the next story.

THE WISHING EGG

"Good morning," said Little Jack Rabbit as the little Yellow Hen opened the door of her tiny green house. "Uncle John and I would like to see your Wishing Egg."

"Who told you I had a Wishing Egg?" she asked, looking sharply at Prof. Jim Crow.

"I did," answered that old black bird, with a twist of his tail.

"You're a meddlesome old person," cackled the little Yellow Hen, "but as long as you're all here, come in," and she led the way to the sitting room. Over in the corner was a nest of nice clean straw, in which lay a big china egg.

"Now you all come here and make a wish," she said, spreading her wings over the egg while she sang very low:

"Wishing Egg, Wishing Egg,Grant three wishes now I beg."

But, oh dear me. For almost a minute and a half neither Little Jack Rabbit nor Uncle John Hare could decide what they wanted. But Prof. Jim Crow could. Oh, my, yes! For all of a sudden in through the window came a silk hat and a swallow tail coat and a big diamond pin.

"Ha, ha!" he laughed, "here are my wishes — one, two, three. Well, now I'm as happy as happy can be," and in less than five hundred short seconds he had them on, silk hat, swallow tail coat and big diamond pin.

"Hurry up and make your wishes," said the little Yellow Hen to the two little bunnies. So Little Jack Rabbit wrinkled his little pink nose and Uncle John Hare shut his eyes, and pretty soon they must have made their wishes for in through the window came a lot of things — a pianograph, a box of lollypops, a gold watch, a Liberty Bond and a fountain pen.

"Now, that's a pretty good day's work," said the old gentleman rabbit with a smile, stroking his whiskers. "But what did you wish for?"

"Nothing at all," answered the little hen. "When you know you can get whatever you want by just wishing you don't want anything. But maybe some day I will, and then I'll wish, never fear." And after that she combed her yellow curls, beg pardon, I mean her feathers — with her red coral comb till she looked prettier than her picture, which hung over the mantelpiece in a red plush frame.

"Some day I hope we'll be able to do you a good turn," said kind Uncle John Hare as he and his little rabbit nephew hopped out to the Bunnymobile. "Any time you are in need call up 'Harebell, one, two, three, Hurray! Turnip City.'"

"Good-by," said the little Yellow Hen, and off they went, but Prof. Jim Crow flew away by himself because he wanted to show his new clothes to Mrs. Crow before supper. And in the next story you shall hear what happened after that.

MAGIC BOOTS

As Little Jack Rabbit and Uncle John Hare rode along in the Bunnymobile, all of a sudden, just like that, they heard someone calling:

"Oh, please come and help me out,I'm caught so tight and fastI haven't seen my dear old homeFor two weeks Sunday last."

"Who can it be?" asked the old gentleman rabbit in a whisper, slowing up the Bunnymobile.

"I don't see anybody," answered his little bunny nephew, "but there must be somebody in trouble, just the same." And then the voice came again, only louder than before:

"Oh, please, oh, please, come rescue me.I'm caught so tight in this old oak tree."

And then, all of a sudden, the two little rabbits saw a tiny dwarf wedged in between a tree and a big rock.

"Wait a minute! We'll see what we can do," and in less than five hundred short seconds Little Jack Rabbit and his uncle were tugging away at the little dwarf and pretty soon they had him out, all except his left foot.

"Slip your foot out of your boot," said the old gentleman rabbit.

"No, that would never do," answered the little man. "If I should do that I would lose my power."

"Are yours magic boots?" asked the old gentleman rabbit, looking down at his own, which he considered about the finest in the world, let me tell you.

"Indeed they are," answered the dwarf, "they are thousand league boots. I can run away from a giant as easily as an automobile from a pushcart."

"Goodness me," exclaimed Uncle John Hare, "they are certainly wonderful. But what are you going to do? Stay fast to that tree all the rest of your life, or walk about like other people?"

Well, this made the dwarf think pretty hard, and by and by he said: "Pull me out and leave the boot. Maybe I can hop on one leg fast enough to get away from a giant anyway." So both little rabbits gave a big tug and out came the dwarf, but the boot was left behind, which made the dwarf quite unhappy until he was asked to take a ride in the Bunnymobile.

"There's an old cobbler who lives near here," said the dwarf. "Perhaps he might make me a boot. I hear he's a very wonderful cobbler." So the two little rabbits set off to find him and soon they came to a hut in the middle of the wood, on the roof of which sat a little robin redbreast singing. But what he said you must wait to hear in the next story.

THE TINY COBBLER

"Tick, tack, twoThe Cobbler makes a shoeThat takes a strideThe whole world wide,Tick, tack, two."

"Did you hear that?" whispered the little dwarf, who in the last story has lost one of his wonderful thousand league boots, you remember. And if you don't, please take my word for it, as there won't be space enough in this story to tell you how it happened.

"Let's go in and ask the price," said Uncle John Hare. So the two little bunnies and the dwarf hopped out of the Bunnymobile and went into the hut. On a wooden bench sat a tiny man dressed in a big leather apron and red-peaked hat, busily making a boot. He didn't seem a bit surprised when the door opened, and he said:

"My little tame robinJust told me that youHave left in a tree,Your thousand league shoe."

"That's right," answered the dwarf. "Will you sell me the one you are making?"

"What will you give me for it?" asked Jim Cobbler, waxing his thread and drawing it carefully through the holes he had just punched in the leather.

"Rubies and diamonds," answered the dwarf, taking a bag from his pocket. "Two diamonds and three rubies, five precious stones, the like of which you have never seen."

"I will finish the boot in a short time," answered Jim Cobbler, "and then you may try it on." And he set to work, and pretty soon, not so very long, it was finished. And would you believe it, it fitted the dwarf perfectly and matched his other boot exactly.

And as soon as he had paid for it, he walked outside and said in a singing way:

"Boots, boots, I would beA thousand miles across the sea."

And, whisk! away he went and was lost to sight before Uncle John Hare could get out his spyglass.

"Well, well," laughed the wonderful shoemaker, coming to the door and shading his eyes with his hand, "it didn't take him long to walk away. Ha! ha! My boots are better than airships." I guess he thought he had done a good day's work, and maybe he had, for two diamonds and three rubies are a fair price for one boot, although it may have a stride of a thousand leagues, more or less.

And just you wait until you hear what happens in the next story.

FIREFLY LANTERNS

Twinkle, twinkle, firefly,Like a diamond in the sky.

Well, it was mighty lucky that this firefly had her tiny lantern along with her, for I don't know how the two little rabbits would have reached home if she hadn't lighted the way for them, for the Bunnymobile lantern had gone out, you see.

"We must buy some new ones," said the old gentleman bunny. "We may be arrested any night, and that would be most unpleasant." So the next morning he and Little Jack Rabbit started off for Bunnyville and by and by, after a while, they crossed the bridge that spanned Rabbit River, which wasn't really much wider than a little brook, and stopped before a hardware store.

"What kind of lanterns have you?" asked Uncle John Hare of the fat Turkey Gobble who kept the store.

"We have Jack lanterns, and miners' lamps, and Japanese lanterns, and — —
"

"That'll do," said the little bunny, "let's see them." And after looking at this and looking at that the old gentleman rabbit picked out two Jack Lanterns.

"These will look scrumptious," he said. "I don't believe another car in town will have one." And then they started off again down the road to see little Ben Meadow.

Now little Ben Meadow lived in a round house.His first name was Ben and his last name was Mouse.

So now you know who little Ben is, but just the same I suppose you wonder why he would be delighted to have two rabbits call on him. Well, I'll tell you. It was because, in the first place, he knew that these two nice bunnies wouldn't hurt him, and in the second place, he wore a collar and belt of leather studded with sharp pointed tacks, which would hurt anyone who tried to catch him.

"Helloa, Ben," said the old gentleman rabbit when the little mouse opened the door. "Have you any green cheese?"

"Maybe, but I'm not sure. It is over two weeks since the Man in the Moon was here," answered Benjamin Meadow Mouse, for that was his whole name, you know, only everybody called him "Ben" for short, and the little mice called him "Bennie."

Pretty soon he came out with a piece of cheese wrapped up in a napkin and handed it to the old gentleman rabbit, who thanked him and said: "I'm going to give a party tonight. You are invited. Come at eight and stay till late," and then he turned the Bunnymobile around and away they went. Pretty soon they passed through the wood, where Bobbie Redvest had his nest.

"Come to my party tonight at eight, bring Mrs. Robin and stay till late," said Uncle John Hare, and in the next story you shall hear what happened after that.

INVITATIONS

You remember in the last story that Uncle John Hare was giving a party and had invited Benjamin Meadow Mouse and Bobbie Redvest, to be there early and stay till late and bring a key to his little front gate.

But now that I come to think of it, I didn't tell you about the key. No, sir, I must have forgotten that. Well, you see, there was a fence all around Uncle John's house, and if you didn't have a key to the little gate, why, of course, you couldn't get in. But the old gentleman rabbit had bought a thousand keys and to every one of his friends had given one, and sometimes two, but not at the same time.

"Now who else shall we invite?" asked the old gentleman bunny, as they rolled along with a laugh and a song.

"Jack Sprite," answered Little Jack Rabbit.

"Of course," laughed the old gentleman bunny, and he turned down the shady dell where the Jack-in-the-pulpit flowers grew, and by and by he came to the one in which Jack lived.

"Oh, yes, I'll come," he said, "and I'll stay late, until the rooster crows at eight."

"All right," answered Uncle John Hare, "I don't care, but don't blame me if I should fall asleep before that time," and then away went the Bunnymobile and before very long the two little rabbits met the little fairy who had once upon a time, not very many stories ago, slept in the old gentleman rabbit's bed.

"Come to my party, come at eight,And bring your key to my little front gate."

"I'll be there, never fear," laughed the little fairy, for Uncle John Hare was noted for his wonderful parties.

"Now that makes three," said Little Jack Rabbit. "Shall we ask the Ragged Rabbit Giant?"

"Sh-s-sh!" whispered the old gentleman bunny, "don't mention his name. I have only ten pounds of cheese for the rarebit. He'd eat a ton at one bite." Then they went on until they met Little Red Riding Hood.

"Come to my party, come at eight,And bring your key to my little front gate."

"I'll be there," answered Little Red Riding Hood, and she ran down to the village to buy a new gown.

"Now who else?" asked the old gentleman rabbit.

"Goodness me, yes, indeed, there's Bo Peep," said Billy Bunny. And in the next story you shall hear about the party.

UNCLE JOHN HARE'S PARTY

You remember we left off in the last story just as the two little rabbits were on their way to ask Bo Peep to come to their party. Well, she said she would, of course, and then Uncle John Hare, the old gentleman bunny, went to the telephone and called up Mother Goose and invited her and all the little people of Mother Goose Land to his party.

"Come to my party, come at eight,And bring your key to my little front gate,"

he added, before hanging up the receiver, for he didn't want anybody to be disappointed, you know. But they would be, just the same, if they forgot to bring their keys, for the old gentleman rabbit would never open his front gate after eight.

"Now we had better hurry home to help Mrs. Daisy Duck get things ready for tonight," and he changed places with his bunny nephew, who took the wheel and steered the Bunnymobile, while kind Uncle John Hare looked over the list of names to make sure no one had been left out, and pretty soon, not so very long, they were home and as busy as could be getting everything ready for the big party.

At eight o'clock, and maybe a few minutes before, the little front gate began to rattle, and Mother Goose came up the walk, followed by Goosey-Goosey-Gander and the Three Blind Mice, who held on to the gander's tail feathers so as not to stub their toes on the front door step.

Then pretty soon, the lock began to rattle again, and in came Jack Sprite and the little Forest Fay, and before 13 minutes past 8 every one was there. Well, by and by it came time to cut the big birthday cake in which was hidden a little gold ring, and of course everyone hoped he would find it in his piece of cake. But of course everybody except Benjamin Meadow Mouse was disappointed, which tells you right away who got the ring.

Now everything was going along as nicely as you please, when, all of a sudden, there came a rap-tap-a-tap at the little front gate, and Mrs. Daisy Duck, the old housekeeper, whispered:

"Somebody's knocking at the gate,We won't let him in because it's too late;No one gets in who has lost his keyNo matter what time the hour may be."

But, goodness me. The knocking kept right on, only louder and louder, and pretty soon a gruff voice said:

"I'm the Ragged Rabbit GiantmanOpen the gate as quick as you can."

"What shall we do?" asked Mrs. Daisy Duck, who was a timid lady duck and never felt safe unless she was out in the middle of Turnip City Lake.

And in the next story, if that big giant doesn't break down the gate, I'll tell you what happened after that.

THE LITTLE RING

"If you don't open the gate, I'll step over the wallIt's not very high, and I'm pretty tall.I guess you had better open the gate;In case I get angry you'll find it too late."

"Oh, dear me!" said Mrs. Daisy Duck, "What shall we do?"

Then what do you suppose little Benjamin Meadow Mouse said? You'd never guess. He ran out of the house, down to the gate, and called out to that great big giant: "Have you a little boy at home?"

"I certainly have," replied the big immense giant rabbit.

"Then take this little ring to him," said Benjamin Meadow Mouse, handing over the ring which he had just found in his piece of birthday cake, as I told you in the last story.

"You are very kind," said the giant. "I'll go home at once and give it to him." And away he went to climb up his mountain.

Well, after that, the birthday party broke up, and all the little guests went home, but before Benjamin Meadow Mouse said good night, Little Jack Rabbit gave him another ring, maybe a little prettier than the one in the birthday cake.

The next morning when Mr. Merry Sun looked into the window he said:

"Wake up, wake up! little boy rabbitDress yourself in your white fur habit.It's going to be a beautiful dayFor I've driven the rain clouds all away."

"That's very nice of you, Mr. Merry Sun," said the little bunny, rubbing his eyes, for he was still sleepy from the birthday party. Then, after a yawn or two, he jumped out of bed, and pretty soon he was downstairs with Uncle John Hare, reading the Bunnyville News.

Well, before very long, they were ready to go for a drive, so they cranked up the Bunnymobile, and started off, and by and by, after a while, and many a mile and a song and a smile, they met little Bobbie Redvest who told them that the Cow That Jumped Over the Moon wasn't feeling very well.

"Goodness me, that's too bad," said the old gentleman bunny. "I guess I'll get the doctor." So off he went, with Little Jack Rabbit, and pretty soon, not so very far, they came to the good doctor's house on the corner of Lettuce Avenue and Pumpkin Square.

And in the next story you shall hear what happened after that.

DOCTOR CAT

Oh, Doctor Cat was very wise,Oh, very wise was he.He knew you'd smile in a little whileIf tickled on the knee.

Well, I hope you remember where we left off in the last story, but in case you don't, Little Jack Rabbit and Uncle John Hare had gone after Doctor Cat to tell him that the Cow That Jumped Over the Moon was ill with the rheumatism.

"That's pretty hard to cure," said the wise cat doctor after the little bunnies had explained matters. "But I will get my little black bag and go with you," and filling it full of little medicine bottles and boxes of pills he put on his coat and hat and followed the two little rabbits out to the Bunnymobile. Then they all started for Mrs. Cow's house in Meadowville, on the corner of Corn Cob Avenue and Clover Street.

"I don't know what will happen if she never can jump over the moon again," said Little Jack Rabbit. "Just think how disappointed all the little boys and girls will be who read Mother Goose. Maybe the Little Dog will never laugh again and the Dish won't run after the Spoon."

"I'll give her a jumping powder," said Dr. Cat. "That's all she needs. Don't worry. I once treated a kangaroo for the same trouble," And he began to purr as if nothing could worry him except, maybe, a big dog.

Well, pretty soon they came to Mrs. Cow's house, so the doctor jumped out and went in. But, oh dear me, Mrs. Cow was sicker than he thought, I guess, for he didn't come out for fifteen minutes, and maybe more.

"How is she?" inquired kind Uncle John Hare when the famous cat doctor was once more seated in the Bunnymobile.

"She hasn't got rheumatism at all," he answered. "She bumped her foot on the edge of the moon, but it will be all well in a few days."

By and by the two little rabbits and the famous cat doctor came to a bridge where they found the old dog who took the toll ill with the flu.

"Let me off here," said Dr. Cat, "and you can go on your way." So the two little bunnies crossed the bridge and stopped at a moving picture theatre.

"There's going to be a show very soon," said a green parrot. "Get your tickets. Don't be late. There won't be a seat by half past eight."

"Shall we go in?" asked the old gentleman rabbit.

And you don't suppose for a minute that Little Jack Rabbit answers "no" in the next story, do you?

THE BIG BLACK BEAR

Now the Moving Picture to which Little Jack Rabbit and Uncle John Hare went in the story before this was about a dog that barked at the moon till the Man in the Moon threw him a bone, after which he sat out in the backyard every night to catch the bones the Man in the Moon threw down to him.

"I wish it had been about the little bird in the Moon Man's house," said Little Jack Rabbit. "I don't care much about dogs."

Well, after that they both jumped into the Bunnymobile and started off for home. But, oh dear me. They had gone only a little way, just so far, when out from the wood jumped a big black bear.

"What are you doing out here by my wood?Your Bunnymobile makes a noiseIt will wake up my cub with its rub-a-dub-dub,And frighten the little bird boys."

"No, it won't," answered the old gentleman rabbit. "Everybody in the Shady Forest knows me. I've taken the fairies out for a drive. They like it."

Well, when the Black Bear heard that he grew more sociable and pretty soon he invited the two little bunnies to call. So Little Jack Rabbit asked him to get in the Bunnymobile, and away they went to the bear's home. And after a while, they saw among the trees a cute little log house.

"That's where I live," said the Black Bear, and in less time than I can take to tell it, they were all out of the Bunnymobile and seated in the parlor.

"Now wait a minute and I'll see if my little cub is awake," said the big Black Bear, and he went to the foot of the stairs to listen.

"Go to sleep, you naughty cub,What makes you wriggle so?You ought to be in Dreamy LandWhere pretty flowers grow."

"Sh-s-sh!" said the big Black Bear, motioning to Uncle John Hare. "Mrs. Bear is singing him to sleep!" So the two little rabbits tiptoed out of the log cabin and hopped into the Bunnymobile, and went softly away, for they knew how hard it is for mothers to get their children to sleep and they didn't want to make trouble for kind Mrs. Bear.

Well, pretty soon these kind little bunnies reached home, where Mrs. Daisy Duck, their housekeeper, stood waiting on the front porch. It was quite late and the Twinkle, Twinkle Star was shining down from the sky. And next time if

The Man in the Moon doesn't lose a centAnd so is unable to pay his rent,

I'll tell you another story about these two little rabbits.

CHICKEN CITY

One morning as Uncle John Hare and his bunny nephew sat on the front porch of their little house on the corner of Turnip Square and Lettuce Avenue they saw a Yellow Hen walking down the road. She had on a pink shawl and a purple sunbonnet and a pair of little red slippers.

"Cackle, cackle, what do you think,I went to the store to buy some ink,Paper and pen a letter to write,But they told me they'd all sold out last night."

"So here I am," said the little Yellow Hen. "I must make you a call," and she hopped up on the porch and sat down in the rocking chair.

"Well, we're glad to see you," said the old gentleman rabbit. "How are all the folks in Chicken City?"

"The old Red Rooster has the chicken pox," she answered. And when the old gentleman rabbit heard that he was dreadfully sorry, for once upon a time that very same rooster used to wake him up every morning for breakfast.

"We'll take the Bunnymobile and go over to see him," he said. And in less than 500 short seconds all three of them were driving toward Chicken City. But, would you believe it, when they reached the old Red Rooster's house they were told he had gone for a walk on the meadow. And pretty soon they heard him say:

"I got over the chickenpox,But I nearly had the fluI'm so glad I'm well again—Cock-a-doodle-do!"

"Too bad you took all this trip for nothing," said the Yellow Hen.

"Not a bit of it," answered the old gentleman bunny. "It's worth going a thousand miles to hear my old friend crow again." And then he and Little Jack Rabbit jumped into the Bunnymobile and started off for home. But they had gone only a little way, maybe a mile and maybe less, when they saw a little pig by the road-side, eating clover tops and wagging his little curly tail to brush away the flies.

"Come, take a ride with us," shouted Little Jack Rabbit. So in jumped the little pig and sat down on the back seat and then the old gentleman bunny made the Bunnymobile go twice as fast to frighten the little pig. But he wasn't scared. He lay back against the nice soft cushions and took a lollypop out of his pocket and made believe he was smoking a pipe. And when the old gentleman rabbit turned around, he nearly upset the Bunnymobile he was so surprised.

And in the next story you shall hear what happened after that.

The Bunnymobile went gliding along,While the two little rabbits sang a song.The little pig now and then joined in,But, oh, dear me! his voice was thin.

"Stop that noise!" cried somebody, all of a sudden, just like that. And from behind a bush a big wildcat jumped right out into the middle of the road. And, oh dear me, again, and maybe once more, but she had dreadful long teeth and sharp pointed claws.

"I won't stop," answered the old gentleman rabbit.

"Yes, you will," said the wildcat, "and what is more I'm going to eat your friend Mr. Pig."

Goodness gracious me! That was a terrible thing to hear, especially if you're a pig. And then with a leap that fierce wildcat landed in the Bunnymobile. But, oh dear me, before she could touch him Little Jack Rabbit picked up a big round rubber tire and threw it over that wicked wildcat's head, and when she tried to get it off the little air valve opened and blew in her eye until she couldn't see anything. And while she had her eyes shut the old gentleman rabbit put a big chain around her waist and padlocked it to the Bunnymobile.

"Now will you be good?" asked Little Jack Rabbit with a grin. "We'll take you to the Catnip City jail and turn you over to the Policeman Dog."

And away went the two little rabbits, but, let me tell you, before they even started the little pig jumped over the seat and sat down beside them, for he didn't want to stay with the big wildcat. Oh, dear no! Not even if she were chained and padlocked.

Well, pretty soon, not so very long, although it seemed a month to the little pig, they came to Catnip City, and in a few minutes after that they stopped in front of the jail.

"What have you got here?" asked the Policeman Dog, coming out with his club in his right paw. "Oh, I see, Mrs. Wildcat. I'm mighty glad you've caught her." And he tickled her ear with his club and locked her up in a cell.

"She won't bother anybody for thirty days," said the Policeman Dog.

And then away went the two little bunnies till they came to a farm where a big turkey gobbler lived.

"Gobble, gobble, gobble!Cried the great big turkey cock.I'd like to find some one to darn,The hole in my purple sock."

"Give it to me and I'll take it home to my housekeeper," said Uncle John Hare. And in the next story you shall hear what happened after that.

PROFESSOR CROW

Now I forgot to tell you in the last story that as soon as the two little rabbits reached the farm where the big Turkey Gobbler had a hole in his purple sock, the little pig jumped out of the Bunnymobile and ran around to the pigsty, and he was in such a hurry that he forgot all about thanking them for the nice ride.

"Now I hope my housekeeper, Mrs. Daisy Duck, has some purple yarn," said the old gentleman rabbit as the Turkey Gobbler handed over the sock with the hole in it, "but if she hasn't I'll get some for her at the One-Two-Three-Cent Store in Turnip City."

"You're very kind," answered the Turkey Gobbler. "Some day I'll do you a favor."

Well, by and by, after a while, the two little rabbits came to a hill which the Bunnymobile wouldn't go up. No, siree. It just stood still and turned its two brass lamps around to see what the old gentleman rabbit was going to do about it.

"Goodness gracious me!" he said. "Now what do you think is the matter. Maybe it wants some gasoline to drink or maybe some milk. I'm sure I don't know which!" And just then Professor Crow flew by and said:

"What is the matter with you, I say;There's a wire stretched across the way,Can't you see it from where you sit?The two front wheels are caught by it."

"So there is," exclaimed Little Jack Rabbit. "Thank you, Professor Crow."

"But how can we cut the wire?" asked the old gentleman rabbit. "I wish Mrs. Daisy Duck were here with her work basket; we could borrow her scissors."

"Ha, ha!" laughed the old black crow. "If you'll give me a ride I'll cut the wire with my beak."

"That will be fine," said Uncle John Hare. "Go ahead and cut it, and then jump in and we'll take you wherever you wish." In a few minutes that clever black bird cut the wire in two, and then the Bunnymobile went up the hill as nicely as you please. And when they reached the top they met a little old man with a pack on his back. He was a very queer looking person, not the least like a dwarf, but much smaller than a boy.

"Take me with you, good friends," he said. "I will reward you with a present from my pack."

"Jump in," said Little Jack Rabbit. "You may sit with Professor Crow on the back seat." So the little old man crawled in, bundle and all, and after a while he undid the string that tied the bag and put his hand inside.

"What shall I pick from out of the bag.Say what you'd like the best.A watch or a ring or a diamond stud,Or a purple velvet vest?"

THE WITCH'S SPELL

Now I guess Little Jack Rabbit and Uncle John Hare, the nice old gentleman bunny, have had plenty of time since I wrote the last story to think what they would rather have from the pack, which the funny little old man had untied as he rode along with them in the Bunnymobile.

"Now tell me what you'd like," he said again.

"I'll take a diamond pin," said the old gentleman rabbit.

"Give me a watch," cried the little bunny.

"A gold ring will suit me," said the little pig. "I can wear it like an earring in my nose."

"I'd like a purple velvet vest," said Prof. Jim Crow; "it will go very nicely with my black swallow-tail coat."

Then the funny little old man pulled out his hand, and, would you believe it? he handed Little Jack Rabbit a diamond pin. And then he put his hand in the bag again and drew out a watch, a ring, and a lovely purple vest.

"Goodness gracious me, but you are generous," said Uncle John Hare. "How can we ever repay you?"

"I will tell you," answered the little old man. "And I hope you will be willing to do what I ask."

"Oh, dear me," thought Little Jack Rabbit, "I know he's going to ask us to do something dangerous."

"In yonder forest," said the little old man, "lives an old witch who keeps in a wicker cage a lovely bird. Now this little bird is really my daughter, but the wicked witch has cast a spell over her. And the only way she can be set free is for someone to touch her with a little blue flower which grows all by itself near a big oak tree, not far from here."

"I will fly away and bring back the flower," said Professor Jim Crow.

"Now then," said the funny little old man, "I will tell you what to do. The little pig must go around to the back of the witch's hut and dig up her garden, and when she runs out to send him away, you two rabbits hop up on the porch and carry off the cage. And as soon as you have it safe in the Bunnymobile, come back to me. I will wait for you here."

Well, by this time, as Prof. Jim Crow had flown after the flower, the two little rabbits and the pig started off for the witch's hut and by and by, after a while, they stopped in the wood and got out. And when they were quite near, the little pig ran around to the back and began to dig up the garden.

Pretty soon, the old witch ran out of the back door to chase the pig and by this time Little Jack Rabbit had placed the birdcage in the Bunnymobile. But, oh dear me. Just as he and his uncle were driving away they heard a dreadful scream, and in the next story I'll tell you what happened after that.

THE MAGIC FLOWER

"Come back, come back with my pretty bird,Or I'll change you both into a snake.How dare you act like a couple of thievesAnd my little pet blue bird take?"

And then the witch gave a dreadful scream, and jumping on her broom-stick flew after Little Jack Rabbit and Uncle John Hare.

Now it may seem strange that a broom-stick can go as fast as a Bunnymobile, but it did, just the same. And maybe a little faster, for pretty soon the old witch was alongside and stretching out her bony hand tried to snatch up the cage with the little blue bird. But just then, all of a sudden, up came Professor Jim Crow with the magic blue flower, and as soon as he touched the little bird she changed into a lovely princess, and the old witch gave another dreadful scream and almost fell off her broom-stick. You see she was afraid of that little magic blue flower, for she knew if she came near it she would turn into a bat, and that would be the end of her. So she flew away on her broom-stick, back to her hut in the wood.

Well, by this time they had reached the funny little old man with his pack who lost no time in touching the little magic flower, when, presto! chango! as the magician says, he turned into a handsome king, and throwing his arms around the princess, cried, "My dearest daughter! At last you are free!" And then he turned to the two little rabbits and Prof. Jim Crow. "How shall I ever repay you?"

"Don't mention it again," said the old gentleman bunny. "We are all glad to have helped you; and besides, you gave us all a present."

Just then the little pig came up, much out of breath, for he had run all the way from the witch's house.

Pretty soon the king and the princess drove off in a great coach drawn by four milk white horses, after saying good-by to the bunnies, the crow and pig. And not so very long, they heard a voice singing:

"My little white dress I have washed so clean,I will iron the ruffles in between,And when the prince comes riding along,I'll sing my prettiest fairy song."

"Who is singing?" asked the little rabbit, and they stopped the Bunnymobile and knocked at the door of a little house they spied in the wood and in less than five seconds, it was opened by a little girl.

"Come in," she said, "I've never seen such nice rabbits before." And in the next story you shall hear what happened after that.

THE RIBBON TREE

In the story before this I told you how a little girl opened the door of her cottage when the two little rabbits went rat-a-tat-tat three times. And you remember she was singing a song about her pretty ruffled dress which she meant to put on before the prince came riding by. Well, as soon as the two little rabbits sat down in the parlor, the little girl said:

"I have a little tree, on which silk ribbons grow;Some are red as roses, some are white as snow.And some are yellow, pink and blue,Come, I'll show my tree to you."

And then she led Little Jack Rabbit and Uncle John Hare into her garden and showed them this wonderful tree. It certainly was a beautiful tree, just covered with little silk ribbons of many colors and on the topmost branch Bobbie Redvest had a nest full of little blue eggs.

And while they stood there admiring this wonderful tree, five little dwarfs ran into the garden and said:

"We want a yard of ribbonAs blue as sunny sky,Two yards of purple colorAnd three of crimson dye."

Then the little girl took a pair of silver scissors from her pocket and clipped off the ribbons. And wasn't it wonderful? No sooner had she cut off a piece than another grew in its place. And after she had rolled up the ribbons in a neat package, the five little dwarfs each took a diamond out of his pocket and gave it to her, and then they hurried away without a word to the two little rabbits.

"They never speak to anyone except in poetry," said the little girl, "and maybe they were too bashful to think of a rhyme for you."

"I'd like to buy a blue ribbon for a tie," said Uncle John Hare.

"I will give you one for nothing," said the little girl, "if you will take me in your Bunnymobile to the One-Two-Three-Cent Store in Catnip City."

"All right," answered Uncle John Hare. So the little girl cut off a piece of blue ribbon and tied it around his neck and then off they went to the One-Two-Three-Cent Store.

"I sell these ribbons for Pussy Cats and Bow-wow Dogs," she said, opening a box which she carried under her arm. "Then I buy groceries and shoes for myself, and some day when the prince comes riding by on his big white horse he will stop to see me, and then maybe he'll ask me to marry him, and I shall be a princess. But I shall take my little magic tree with me and plant it in the castle garden, for it is my lucky charm." And in the next story, just wait until you hear what happens.

THE FAIRY CAT

When the two little rabbits and the little girl reached the One-Two-Three-Cent Store in Catnip City, they all jumped out of the Bunnymobile. Now, I don't believe I ever told you about the One-Two-Three-Cent Store. It was kept by a Fairy Cat, whose name was Tabby Tiny Cat. And all the fairies for miles around bought things at her store, for she kept every kind of a thing—candies made of honey dew, nuts and maple sugar, Sunbeam Taffy and Moonlight Marshmallows, as well as Cobweb Laces and pretty moss rugs and Sugar Maple Icicle Candy.

"Come in, come in," said the Fairy Cat.

"I've things for a penny and some for two, and others for three, now what will it be?"

"Let me look around first," said Little Jack Rabbit. "Mrs. Daisy Duck, my uncle's housekeeper, makes all the good things we want to eat, but maybe you will have something we'd like to buy." So while he and Uncle John Hare looked around, the little girl showed the lovely Magic Tree Ribbons to the Fairy Cat who said:

"I'll take them all, for the Fairy Cats will need bows for Easter." Then the little girl bought flour and sugar and a pair of little red shoes, and a dainty sunbonnet with a yellow butterfly on it. And then she was ready to go home. But the two little rabbits were still looking around trying to find something which they could buy for Mrs. Daisy Duck.

Pretty soon a Yellow Bird in a wicker cage began to sing:

"Buy a fairy dewdrop pinYour purple tie to fasten in."

"Good," said Uncle John Hare, "that's what I want."

"Buy a silver tick-tock watchTo tell the time of day.You'll find it very usefulWhen riding miles away,"

sang the little bird.

"That's the very thing," exclaimed Little Jack Rabbit. And as soon as they had paid the Fairy Cat, they all jumped into the Bunnymobile and started back for the little girl's house where in the garden grew the Magic Ribbon Tree I told you about in the last story.

But, oh dear me. Just as they drew up at the front gate, they saw the Ragged Rabbit Giant behind the house. "Oh, dear," said the little girl. "He will pick off all the lovely ribbons. What shall I do?"

Well, just then, all of a sudden, a big tremendous long snake crawled out from behind a tree. And in the next story, you shall hear what happened after that.

THE BIG BLACK SNAKE

"I'm as strong as an iron ropeI can bind a giant fast;If I coil like a belt around his waist,I can make him breathe his last,"

sang the Big Black Snake just as I finished the last story.

"Then help us," said Little Jack Rabbit, "for the Ragged Rabbit Giant is picking all the lovely ribbons from the little girl's magic tree."

"Keep quiet," said the snake, "and I will glide around into the garden and see what I can do."

So Uncle John Hare, Little Jack Rabbit and the little girl hid behind a lilac bush. And pretty soon, not so very long, they heard a dreadful noise. Oh, dear me, yes. And in another minute the Ragged Rabbit Giant ran out of the garden with the big snake coiled about his waist.

Now the Ragged Rabbit Giant was tremendously strong, and the snake found it hard work to squeeze the breath out of him. But, just the same, Ragged Rabbit Giant was mighty uncomfortable, let me tell you. And pretty soon he said in a whisper:

"If you will tell this dreadful snakeTo bother me no more,I'll never pass this way againNor knock upon your door."

"Shall I let him go?" asked the snake, winking his left eye at Uncle John Hare. "First make him give us a promise," answered the wise old gentleman rabbit. So the big bunny giant made a solemn vow never to bother them again.

"You are a very kind snake," said the little girl, "I will give you some ribbons for your children's Easter bonnets." And she ran into the garden and with her silver scissors clipped off some pretty ribbons and gave them to the snake, who then glided away to his home.

Just then the sound of a bugle was heard and the little girl cried:

"Here comes the prince on his snow-white steedAs my godmother told me he would,To take me away to his castle gayIn the midst of the whispering wood."

And sure enough, in a few minutes the prince came by and asked the little girl to come to his castle. So she pulled up the Magic Ribbon Tree and locked the door of her little house, and then the handsome prince lifted her up on the saddle and rode away to the castle. And as soon as the little girl was seated behind him she grew into a beautiful young princess. And in the next story, oh, just wait until you hear what happens.

THE SUGAR BARREL

Said Mrs. Daisy Duck one day,"The sugar all has gone awayThe ants have made a call I fear,And taken it away from here."

"Never mind," said Uncle John Hare, the old gentleman rabbit, "perhaps they couldn't buy any lollypops at the One-Two-Three-Cent Store."

"But what am I to do?" asked Mrs. Daisy Duck. "I must have sugar to make Angel cake."

"If that's the case," said the old gentleman bunny, "I'll motor over to Turnip City and buy some." So he and Little Jack Rabbit jumped into the Bunnymobile and away they went, and after a while, and maybe a mile, and a laugh and a smile, they stopped at the Big Grocery Store.

Now the manager of the sugar department was a very nice pig, and when he advised Uncle John Hare to take a barrel of sugar instead of three pounds for twenty-five cents, the old gentleman rabbit said all right, he would. But, goodness me. They had a dreadful time getting that heavy barrel into the Bunnymobile. But after a while they rolled it up on the back seat, and then they started off for home. But, goodness me again! They had gone but a little way when, all of a sudden, just like that, a voice sang out:

"What have you got in that barrelThat sits up so straight on the seat.You'd have a close call if it happened to fallOn top of your four little feet."

"Who are you?" asked the old gentleman bunny, stopping the Bunnymobile and looking all about him. But he couldn't see anybody, and neither could the little rabbit, although he put up his spyglasses and looked over the top of a tall oak tree.

"Here I am," said the voice, and all of a sudden, just like that, a big honey bee flew out of a flower.

"Ha, ha!" laughed the old gentleman rabbit, "I guess you smelt sugar. We have enough in that barrel to last for maybe a year and a day, as they say in Fairy Land."

"I will give you a box of honey for two pounds of sugar," said the bee. "Mr. Bee told me this morning that he was tired of honey in his coffee."

"Get in the Bunnymobile and come with us," said the old gentleman bunny.
"When we get there I'll open the barrel and give you some." So away they
went and soon they came across an old rag doll lying in the dusty road.

"Goodness me," exclaimed the old gentleman rabbit, "she must have
fainted." And, sure enough, this was the case, for as soon as she was lifted
into the Bunnymobile she opened her eyes and said: "In the next story I'll
tell you how I was lost by a little girl with a blue sunbonnet."

THE YELLOW DOG TRAMP

"I'm a plain rag doll in a dress of blue,And I've been lost, an hour or twoBy a little girl with a curly headWho will cry for me when she goes to bed."

This is what the Rag Doll said to the two little rabbits who picked her up in the last story, you remember.

"Dear me!" exclaimed the old gentleman bunny. "What's the name of the little girl?"

"Lucy Locket," said the Rag Doll. And then Little Jack Rabbit began to laugh, for he had once read of a little Lucy Locket who had lost her pocket, and he remembered that she lived not far away. So he steered the Bunnymobile while the old gentleman bunny talked to the Rag Doll, and by and by, not so very long, they came to a pretty house, and right there on the front porch sat a little girl crying.

"Hello, don't cry; wipe your eye!" shouted kind Uncle John Hare. "We have found your rag dolly!" And in another minute the Rag Dolly was in the little girl's arms.

"Good-by," said the two little rabbits, and they drove away to find another adventure, and pretty soon they found one. Oh, my yes! The Yellow Dog Tramp came out of the wood and said:

"I've been tramping, tramping, trampingFor many a weary mile;Across the way, through fields of hay,And through the old turnstile.Oh, won't you take me for a ride?I've a dreadful pain in my poor old side."

"Jump in," said the old gentleman rabbit with a kind smile. "You're not the kind of a dog who bothers little bunnies."

"No, I'm not," answered the Yellow Dog Tramp, "I'd like to find a nice home and stay there."

"Well, you come with us," said the little bunny. "You can clean the Bunnymobile and work in the garden."

"Hurrah!" barked the Yellow Dog Tramp. "I feel like a boy again already, I used to do those things before I became a hobo doggy."

Well, by this time they were almost home, and in less than five hundred more short seconds they were in the garage where the old gentleman rabbit fixed up a little room for the Yellow Dog Tramp, with a looking glass at one end and a little white bed at the other.

"Now you brush your coat and trousers and part your hair in the middle and then come in to supper," said the old gentleman rabbit. And in the next story you shall hear what happened after that.

"ALWAYS TRUST THE FAIRIES"

Uncle John's little gardenIs full of bright flowersAnd the fairies play tagThrough all the bright hours.

"Dear me," said the Yellow Dog Tramp, to himself, peeping out of the garage, where we left him in the last story, "they seem to be having a fine time!" And he sighed, for he was thinking of another garden up in Vermont and the old farm where he was a boy, long ago, before he had run away from home.

"Who's eye is watching us?" cried one of the fairies, all of a sudden, just like that. And then, of course, all these little people stopped playing but they couldn't see anything but the Yellow Dog Tramp's right eye, which, I forgot to tell you, was peeping through a tiny knothole.

"The Yellow Dog Tramp, who is old and lameIs watching you play your tag-a-rag game,"

he answered, whereupon all the fairies said:

"Jump over the fence, and play awhileDrop your scowl and put on a nice smile."

And when the Yellow Dog Tramp heard that, he couldn't help but laugh, and in less than five hundred short seconds he was over the wall. But, oh dear me. In a few minutes the big Ragged Rabbit Giant leaned over the tree top and said in a deep gruff voice:

"Fee, fum, fag, fog.I smell the blood of a yellow dog."

"Quick, I must change you into a fairy puppy," said the queen fairy, and she waved her bright wand, and in less time than I can take to tell it he became small enough to creep into a tulip flower.

"Where has that dog gone?" asked the big Ragged Rabbit Giant, peeking under the bushes and behind the sunflowers, but he never thought to look in the tulip.

"Thunder and lightning! What happened to that dog," and the Giant Rabbit dusted off the knees of his trousers after creeping under a lilac bush; "he must be here somewhere." But not a fairy said a word, and pretty soon a mosquito stung that wicked old Giant Rabbit on the back of his neck, which made him so angry that he stepped over the garden wall and walked away.

And when he was out of sight the queen fairy changed the Yellow Dog Tramp back again into his natural shape:

"Always trust the fairiesIf danger you are in.And always say 'A lucky day!'When e'er you find a pin,"

sang the queen fairy as the happy Yellow Dog Tramp ran into Uncle John Hare's little house.

And there we will leave him for the present, but in another book, entitled "Little Jack Rabbit and Professor Crow," you'll hear more about the little rabbits and their friends.

THE END